CINCINNATI
BENGALS

BY JOSH ANDERSON

Stride
An Imprint of The Child's World®
childsworld.com

Published by The Child's World®
800-599-READ • www.childsworld.com

Copyright © 2023 by The Child's World®
All rights reserved. No part of this book
may be reproduced or utilized in any form
of by any means without written permission
from the publisher.

Photography Credits
Cover: © Justin Casterline / Stringer / Getty Images; page 1: © Africa Studio / Shutterstock; page 3: © Rob Carr / Staff / Getty Images; page 5: © Justin Berl / Stringer / Getty Images; page 6: © Sean P Bender / Wikimedia; page 9: © Michael Hickey / Stringer / Getty Images; page 10: © John Grieshop / Stringer / Getty Images; page 11: © stevezmina1 / Getty Images; page 12: © Andy Lyons / Staff / Getty Images; page 12: © Greg Fiume / Stringer / Getty Images; page 13: © Associated Press / AP; page 13: © Jamie Sabau / Stringer / Getty Images; page 14: © Michael Hickey / Stringer / Getty Images; page 15: © Andy Lyons / Staff / Getty Images; page 16: © Getty Images / Staff / Getty Images; page 16: © Jonathan Daniel / Stringer / Getty Images; page 17: © Joe Murphy / Stringer / Getty Images; page 17: © Kirk Irwin / Stringer / Getty Images; page 18: © Associated Press / AP; page 18: © Stephen Dunn / Staff / Getty Images; page 19: © John Grieshop / Stringer / Getty Images; page 19: © Staff / Getty Images; page 20: © John Grieshop / Stringer / Getty Images; page 20: © Jason Miller / Stringer / Getty Images; page 21: © Andy Lyons / Staff / Getty Images; page 21: © Andy Lyons / Staff / Getty Images; page 22: © Lachlan Cunningham / Stringer / Getty Images; page 23: © Rick Stewart / Stringer / Getty Images; page 23: © stevezmina1 / Getty Images; page 25: © David Eulitt / Stringer / Getty Images; page 26: © Handout / Getty Images; page 29: © Vincent Laforet / Staff / Getty Images

ISBN Information
9781503857759 (Reinforced Library Binding)
9781503860445 (Portable Document Format)
9781503861800 (Online Multi-user eBook)
9781503863163 (Electronic Publication)

LCCN 2021952661

Printed in the United States of America

TABLE OF CONTENTS

Go Bengals! 4
Becoming the Bengals 6
By the Numbers 8
Game Day 10
Uniform 12
Team Spirit 14
Heroes of History 16
Big Days 18
Modern-Day Marvels 20
The GOAT 22
The Big Game 24
Amazing Feats 26
All-Time Best 28

Glossary 30
Find Out More 31
Index and About the Author 32

GO BENGALS!

The Cincinnati Bengals compete in the National Football **League's** (NFL) American Football Conference (AFC). They play in the AFC North **division**, along with the Baltimore Ravens, Cleveland Browns, and Pittsburgh Steelers. The Steelers are the Bengals' biggest rival. When the Bengals and Steelers play, it's always a big game! The Bengals have played in three **Super Bowls** in their history, but they haven't won the big game yet. Let's learn more about the Bengals!

AFC NORTH DIVISION

Baltimore Ravens

Cincinnati Bengals

Cleveland Browns

Pittsburgh Steelers

THE BENGALS HAVE WORN WHITE, ORANGE, AND BLACK SINCE 1968, THEIR FIRST YEAR IN THE NFL.

BECOMING THE BENGALS

Long before the Bengals, there were other professional football teams in Cincinnati. But none of the teams lasted more than a few seasons before shutting down. The Bengals joined the American Football League (AFL) in 1968, two seasons before the AFL and NFL merged to form one league. Paul Brown was the team's original owner and head coach. Brown named the team the "Bengals" after one of the earlier Cincinnati teams from the 1930s and 1940s.

BEFORE HIS PRO CAREER, PAUL BROWN COACHED AT MASSILLON WASHINGTON HIGH SCHOOL IN MASSILLON, OHIO. A STATUE OF BROWN STANDS OUTSIDE OF THE SCHOOL.

BY THE NUMBERS

The Bengals have played in **THREE** Super Bowls.

TEN division titles for the Bengals

460 points scored by the team in 2021—a Bengals record!

57 straight sold-out home games for the Bengals from 2003 to 2010

WIDE RECEIVER A. J. GREEN SCORED 65 TOUCHDOWNS DURING HIS NINE SEASONS WITH THE BENGALS.

PLAYER INTRODUCTIONS AT PAUL BROWN STADIUM GET FANS EXCITED FOR THE UPCOMING GAME.

GAME DAY

The Bengals have played their home games at Paul Brown **Stadium** in downtown Cincinnati since 2000. Before that, the team shared a stadium with the Cincinnati Reds, a Major League Baseball team. On game days, Paul Brown Stadium holds about 65,000 fans. Fans and players often face chilly temperatures during the winter. A 2007 game against the Bengals' biggest rival set the stadium's attendance record. The Pittsburgh Steelers defeated the Bengals 24–13 in front of 66,188 fans.

We're Famous!

The Bengals can count George Clooney as one of their biggest fans. Clooney even stood up for the team on the red carpet at the Oscars when he ran into Ed Reed, a player for the Baltimore Ravens. Clooney engaged Reed in some good-natured trash talk over the Ravens–Bengals division rivalry.

UNIFORM

BLACK

WHITE

Truly Weird

The AFC Championship Game between the Bengals and the San Diego Chargers on January 10, 1982, is nicknamed "The Freezer Bowl." The temperature during that game reached −9 degrees Fahrenheit (−23 degrees Celsius). Even in the bitter cold, the Bengals' offensive linemen decided not to wear long sleeves under their jerseys that day. Their ice-cold decision paid off. The Bengals won 27–7 and earned a trip to the Super Bowl.

Alternate Jersey

Sometimes teams wear an alternate jersey that is different from their home and away jerseys. It might be a bright color or have a unique theme. The Bengals wore orange jerseys for a December 2020 game against the rival Pittsburgh Steelers. Wearing the bright jerseys, the Bengals came out on top 27–17.

FOR BENGALS FANS, SHOUTING "WHO DEY!" DURING A GAME MEANS THE SAME AS YELLING "GO BENGALS!"

TEAM SPIRIT

Going to a game at Paul Brown Stadium can be loads of fun! Since 1980, fans have enjoyed a chant that goes, "Who dey, who dey, who dey think gonna beat dem Bengals?" Together the crowd answers, "Nobody!" The chant is so popular that the team's mascot, a costumed tiger, is named Who Dey. Who Dey and the Ben-Gals cheerleaders also can be found on the sideline at every game rooting on the team. And don't miss the Who Dey Melt at the stadium—a grilled cheese with macaroni and bacon inside!

WHO DEY

HEROES OF HISTORY

Ken Anderson
Quarterback | 1971–1986

Anderson is the Bengals' all-time leader in passing yards, with 32,838. He won the 1981 **Most Valuable Player** (MVP) Award and played 16 seasons for the Bengals. That's more than any other player. Anderson led the team to its first Super Bowl appearance after the 1981 season.

Geno Atkins
Defensive Tackle | 2010–2020

For 11 seasons, Atkins anchored the Bengals' defensive line. He helped lead the team to the **playoffs** four times during that stretch. Atkins had 75.5 **sacks** with the team, which is third most in franchise history. He was selected for the Pro Bowl eight times.

Boomer Esiason
Quarterback | 1984–1992, 1997

Four-time **Pro Bowler** Esiason was the team's starting quarterback for eight seasons. In 1988, after leading the Bengals to the Super Bowl, Esiason won the MVP Award. He ranked in the top ten in passing **touchdowns** during seven different seasons.

Chad Johnson
Wide Receiver | 2001–2010

The Bengals' all-time leading receiver earned six trips to the Pro Bowl during his career. In 2006, Johnson led the league with 1,369 yards receiving. As a Bengal, he caught 66 touchdowns. Johnson wore number 85 on the field and was nicknamed "Ochocinco," which means "85" in Spanish.

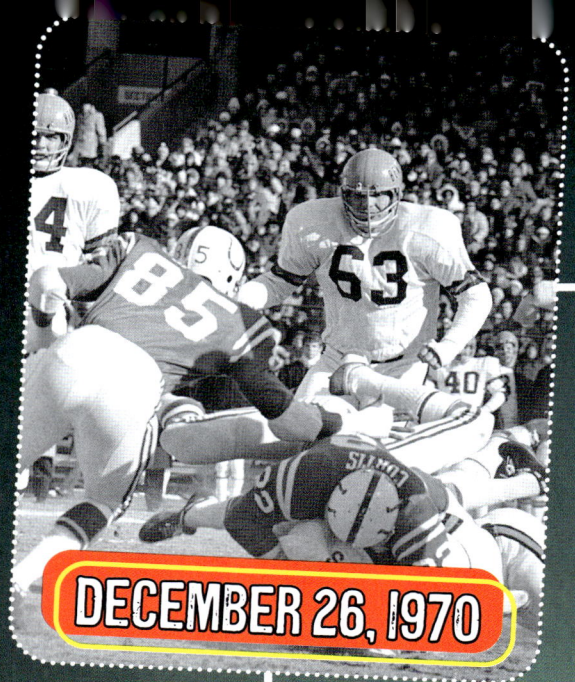

DECEMBER 26, 1970

The Bengals compete in their first-ever playoff game. They fall to the Baltimore Colts 17–0.

Ickey Woods runs for two touchdowns in the AFC Championship Game. The Bengals defeat the Buffalo Bills 21–10 and go to the Super Bowl for the second time ever.

JANUARY 8, 1989

BIG DAYS

JANUARY 3, 2016

The Bengals defeat the Baltimore Ravens 24–16 for their twelfth win of the season, tying a franchise record.

The Bengals have the first choice of the 2020 NFL Draft. The team picks Joe Burrow, hoping he will be the franchise quarterback of the future.

APRIL 23, 2020

MODERN-DAY MARVELS

Jessie Bates III
Safety | Debut: 2018

Bates led the team in tackles as a **rookie** and never looked back. He helped anchor the Cincinnati pass defense in 2020, which held opponents to only a 62.8 percent pass completion rate. Bates started every game during his first three seasons, and he played in nearly 99 percent of all defensive snaps.

Joe Burrow
Quarterback | Debut: 2020

Burrow began his rookie season on fire. He completed 264 passes in his first ten games. That's more than any rookie in NFL history. Burrow was also the first rookie to ever throw for 300 yards in three straight games. In 2021, Burrow led the Bengals to the third Super Bowl in team history.

Ja'Marr Chase
Wide Receiver | Debut: 2021

Chase was the Bengals' first-round draft pick in 2021. The Bengals made him the fifth-overall pick after a very successful college career at Louisiana State University. Chase had an incredible rookie season in 2021, finishing with 1,455 receiving yards and 13 touchdowns. He was chosen for the Pro Bowl as a rookie.

Joe Mixon
Running Back | Debut: 2017

Since joining the Bengals in 2017, Mixon has provided electricity to the team's ground game. He led the team in rushing as a rookie. Mixon has rushed for more than 1,000 yards three times. He scored 33 touchdowns in his first five seasons. Mixon was selected for his first Pro Bowl after the 2021 season.

LEGENDARY OFFENSIVE LINEMAN ANTHONY MUÑOZ WORE THE NUMBER 78 DURING HIS ENTIRE CAREER WITH THE BENGALS.

THE GOAT
GREATEST OF ALL TIME

ANTHONY MUÑOZ

Muñoz is considered one of the greatest offensive linemen in the history of football. His skill as a blocker was key to helping the Bengals reach two Super Bowls. He was chosen for the Pro Bowl for 11 straight seasons from 1981 to 1991. Muñoz is the only player who spent most of his career as a Bengal to be enshrined in the Pro Football **Hall of Fame**.

FAN FAVORITE
Ickey Woods–Fullback
1988–1991

Woods became a beloved figure in Cincinnati for his end zone dance called the "Ickey Shuffle." Woods would do the dance after he scored a touchdown. In 1988, Woods tied for second in the league with 15 touchdowns, so he had plenty of occasions to perform for the fans.

THE BIG GAME

JANUARY 30, 2022 – AFC CHAMPIONSHIP GAME

The Bengals reached the AFC Championship Game for the first time in more than 30 years. Their opponent was the Kansas City Chiefs. After the first half, the Chiefs led the game 21-3. By the end of the third quarter, the Bengals had battled back and tied the game 21-21. The Bengals took a 24-21 lead on a field goal with about six minutes left, but the Chiefs tied the game just as time ran out. The Bengals' defense stopped Kansas City from scoring in overtime, and kicker Evan McPherson won the game for Cincinnati with a field goal. With the 27-24 victory, the Bengals earned a trip to Super Bowl 56.

QUARTERBACK JOE BURROW THREW TWO TOUCHDOWN PASSES AS HE LED THE BENGALS TO VICTORY OVER THE KANSAS CITY CHIEFS.

PAUL BROWN WAS THE FIRST COACH IN BENGALS HISTORY. HE COACHED THE TEAM FOR EIGHT SEASONS.

AMAZING FEATS

34 Touchdown Passes — In 2021 by QUARTERBACK Joe Burrow

13.5 Sacks — In 2015 by DEFENSIVE END Carlos Dunlap

15 Rushing Touchdowns — In 1988 by FULLBACK Ickey Woods

10,783 Career Receiving Yards — By WIDE RECEIVER Chad Johnson

ALL-TIME BEST

PASSING YARDS

Ken Anderson
32,838

Andy Dalton
31,594

Boomer Esiason
27,149

RUSHING YARDS

Corey Dillon
8,061

James Brooks
6,447

Rudi Johnson
5,742

RECEIVING YARDS

Chad Johnson
10,783

A. J. Green
9,430

Isaac Curtis
7,101

SACKS*

Eddie Edwards
84.5

Carlos Dunlap
82.5

Geno Atkins
75.5

SCORING

Jim Breech
1,151

Shayne Graham
779

Mike Nugent
718

INTERCEPTIONS

Ken Riley
65

Louis Breeden
33

David Fulcher
31

*unofficial before 1982

IN ADDITION TO LEADING THE BENGALS IN RUSHING YARDS, COREY DILLON SCORED 50 TOUCHDOWNS DURING HIS SEVEN SEASONS IN CINCINNATI.

GLOSSARY

division (dih-VIZSH-un): a group of teams within the NFL who play each other more frequently and compete for the best record

Hall of Fame (HAHL of FAYM): a museum in Canton, Ohio, that honors the best players in NFL history.

league (LEEG): an organization of sports teams that compete against each other

Most Valuable Player (MOHST VAL-yoo-bul PLAY-uhr): a yearly award given to the top player in the NFL

playoffs (PLAY-ahfs): a series of games after the regular season that decides which two teams play in the Super Bowl

Pro Bowl (PRO BOWL): the NFL's All-Star game where the best players in the league compete

rookie (RUH-kee): a player playing in his first season

sack (SAK): when a quarterback is tackled behind the line of scrimmage before he can throw the ball

stadium (STAY-dee-uhm): a building with a field and seats for fans where teams play

Super Bowl (SOO-puhr BOWL): the championship game of the NFL, played between the winners of the AFC and the NFC

touchdown (TUTCH-down): a play in which the ball is brought into the other team's end zone, resulting in six points

FIND OUT MORE

IN THE LIBRARY

Bulgar, Beth and Mark Bechtel. *My First Book of Football*. New York, NY: Time Inc. Books, 2015.

Jacobs, Greg. *The Everything Kids' Football Book, 7th Edition*. Avon, MA: Adams Media, 2021.

Sports Illustrated Kids. *The Greatest Football Teams of All Time*. New York, NY: Time Inc. Books, 2018.

Wyner, Zach. *Cincinnati Bengals*. New York, NY: AV2, 2020.

ON THE WEB

Visit our website for links about the Cincinnati Bengals:
childsworld.com/links

Note to parents, teachers, and librarians: We routinely verify our web links to make sure they are safe and active sites. Encourage your readers to check them out!

INDEX

American Football Conference (AFC) 4, 13, 18, 24
Anderson, Ken 16, 28
Atkins, Geno 16, 28

Bates, Jessie, III 20
Ben-Gals 15
Brown, Paul 7, 26
Burrow, Joe 19–20, 25, 27

Chase, Ja'Marr 21
Clooney, George 11

Esiason, Boomer 17, 28

Freezer Bowl 13

Johnson, Chad 17, 27–28

McPherson, Evan 24
Mixon, Joe 21
Muñoz, Anthony 22–23

Paul Brown Stadium 10–11, 15

Who Dey 14–15
Woods, Ickey 18, 23, 27

ABOUT THE AUTHOR

Josh Anderson has published over 50 books for children and young adults. His two boys are the greatest joys in his life. Hobbies include coaching his sons in youth basketball, no-holds-barred games of Apples to Apples, and taking long family walks. His favorite NFL team is a secret he'll never share!